the happiness of kati

the happiness of kati

Jane Vejjajiva

ATHENEUM BOOKS FOR YOUNG READERS

New York   London   Toronto   Sydney

Atheneum Books for Young Readers
An imprint of Simon & Schuster Children's Publishing Division
1230 Avenue of the Americas
New York, New York 10020
Originally published in Thai in 2003 by Preaw Juvenile Books/
Amarin Printing and Publishing Public Company, Ltd., Thailand.
Book design by Yaffa Jaskoll
The text for this book is set in Berkeley Book.
Manufactured in the United States of America
First U.S. Edition 2006
10 9 8 7 6 5 4 3 2 1
Library of Congress Cataloging-in-Publication Data
Vejjajiva, Jane.
The happiness of Kati/ Jane Vejjajiva; translated by Prudence Borthwick.
p. cm.
Summary: With the impending death of her mother, Kati, a young Thai
girl, completes the puzzle of her past and discovers the reason why her
mother gave her up as a baby.
ISBN-13: 978-1-4169-1788-5
ISBN-10: 1-4169-1788-8
[1. Mothers and daughters—Fiction. 2. Amyotrophic lateral sclerosis—
Fiction.] I. Title
PZ7.V48725Hap 2006
[Fic]—dc22
2005024210

PART 1

The Home on the Water

1

Pan and Spatula
Mother never promised to return.

The clatter of the spatula against the pan woke Kati that morning as it had every morning she could remember. The warm scent of freshly cooked rice also played a part, not to mention the smoke from the stove and the smell of crispy fried eggs. But it was the sound of the spatula hitting the side of the pan that finally broke into Kati's slumber and roused her from her dreams.

Kati never took long to wash her face and get dressed, and Grandpa joked that she just waved at the washbasin as she raced past. Grandma turned to look at Kati when she came into the kitchen. Grandma seldom smiled or greeted her. Grandpa said Grandma's smiles were so rare they should be preserved and canned for export overseas, like top-quality produce.

Kati ladled rice into a silver bowl. The white of the rice matched the freshness of the morning air as she cradled the rice bowl against her. The warm steam seemed to rise and fill her chest and her heart, which began to beat faster and harder as she set off at a run for the pier. Grandpa was already waiting there—reading his newspaper, as always. A tray—containing curry, vegetables, and fried fish, each dish in a small plastic bag—was beside him. With the addition of Kati's steaming bowl of rice, their daily merit offering to the monks was complete.

Before long came the sound of oars slapping the water, and the bow of a boat appeared round the bend. The vermilion robes of the venerable abbot added a flash of color to the morning. The abbot's pupil and nephew, Tong, flashed his teeth in a smile that could be seen from afar. Grandpa said Tong should join an acting troupe and go into comedy theater, his smile was so contagious. Tong's smiles came straight from his cheerful heart, made for his lips and glistening eyes, and sent out ripples like a stone dropped in a pool, so that people around him were affected too.

Under the big banyan tree, Grandpa poured water from a little brass vessel onto the ground, completing the offering to the monks. Like a river flowing from the mountains to the sea, the water symbolized the merit they had earned and passed on to departed loved ones. Kati joined her prayers to Grandpa's and prayed silently that her own wishes would be granted.

Breakfast was waiting for them at home. They had a big meal like this every morning. Grandpa took the boiled vegetables with the pungent chili sauce, leaving the stir-fried vegetables and fried fish almost entirely to Kati. Grandpa avoided fried foods of all kinds. He complained behind Grandma's back that eating Grandma's cooking was like eating everything coated in varnish, and that one day he would donate Grandma's pan and spatula to the army to melt down for a cannon for King and Country. If Grandma heard him, she'd make such a racket with her spatula and pan that it was a miracle they were still able to do their duty afterward.

2

The Lunch Container
Kati waited every day for Mother.

Kati loved her tin lunch container. Grandpa called it the "food-mobile," and it was compact yet held just enough food to fill you up nicely. Grandma didn't want to see leftover food brought home to rot, and she knew exactly the capacity of Kati's stomach. Grandma's lunch menu never missed the mark, not with ever-tasty minced basil-and-chili chicken with a fried egg on top; or boiled eggs, rich brown because they'd soaked up the aniseed gravy overnight; or crispy fried "son-in-law" eggs with their sweet-and-sour tamarind sauce; or smooth and creamy steamed egg custard; or quail eggs dipped in batter and fried. Grandpa called Kati an "eggivore," for as long as the lunch menu included eggs, there was never any need to coax Kati to eat—she would devour the lot every time.

Every school morning the bus would stop to pick up Kati. The route of the little open buses ran past the mouth of the lane leading to their house, so she would wait for the bus at this spot. Grandpa would give Kati a lift there on the back of his bicycle. Kati liked hanging tightly on to Grandpa's back. She liked the smell of his cologne that came from the bottle with the sailing ship on it. She liked the little breeze that dried away her sweat. The bus would be crowded with children because it was only a short way to the school, and Grandpa would call out for the passengers to make room for Kati and would tell Uncle Loh to drive slowly and not to lurch about. "You're taking them to school, not driving in the Grand Prix, so make sure you don't end up spilling them out the back in a heap," Grandpa instructed, but Uncle Loh just laughed in reply.

The children put their lunch containers in the dining hall before putting their bags away in the schoolrooms. The lunch containers stood together, big and small, tall and short, and many different colors. They probably conversed about the food they each contained, how tasty and spicy their food was and who had cooked it, and whether the rice had been served out lovingly or only dutifully. Did they hold just enough cold leftovers to fill the owner's stomach, or the most delicious secret recipe from a market stall so popular the stallholder could hardly dish out the food fast enough? Some containers had a sticky rim, still unwashed from the day before. Some had ants. Some were battered and dented, because they'd been handed down many times. Finally, the lunch containers would probably whisper about that really flash lunch container and whether she would turn up to strut her stuff as usual.

Flash was the air-conditioned car, which drove up to wait in front of the school. Flash was the lunch container who came with the maid wearing a uniform like a servant of some aristocratic family. Flash were the embossed designs on that lunch container, which would open to reveal piping hot rice, steaming clear broth, and exotic dishes the other lunch containers never knew about because they never had the chance to discuss these things with the flash lunch container. She only arrived at the school just before lunch break and was whisked away with the start of the first period of the afternoon.

The school bell clanged for lunch break. Kati raced her friends downstairs and ran past Tong walking in the opposite direction. Tong was three years older than Kati and in Year Seven at school. Tong smiled at her before he left on his way home to the temple. Tong said that at lunchtime he had a whole buffet meal waiting for him from the varied offerings people had made to the monks.

In the afternoon, when Kati got home from

school, she washed her lunch container and placed the sections to drain in a basin in the kitchen. Later, in the evening, she would dry them and put them by the stove, handy for Grandma in the morning. Perhaps at night the lunch container would strike up a conversation with the stove to pass the lonely hours, asking how Grandma spent her day, and if she did anything else but get angry with Grandpa.

3

The Washtubs and the Pegs
In the house there were no photos of Mother.

Kati's job was to take the clothes from the line and put them in the washtub for Grandma to sort. This had been her chore even when she was too small to reach the clothes pegs on the line. Grandpa had made her a little set of moveable steps with a basket attached to hold the tub. He would push Kati and the steps slowly between the clotheslines. The wind blew, and the clothes waved and shook with the wind, fluttering wildly, filling with air and straining against the colored clothes pegs like birds that spread their wings but could not fly away.

The clothes pegs had been plain wooden ones when they were bought, but Kati had colored them with crayons, pencils, and paint progressively, as she mastered each medium. It had started one day when Grandpa said that as a young man he had been a children's art teacher. The funny look that came over Grandma's face only encouraged Grandpa to go on about primary colors, warm and cool colors, complementary and opposite colors. He finished by reaching for the nearest object on which to demonstrate his skill. That day the clothes pegs had been right beside him.

The moveable stairs reflected Kati's height. Now, at the age of nine, she needed only the first step to reach the line. But Kati liked to climb up so that she was higher than the clothesline. She would move her arms like a music conductor, like Mickey Mouse in *Fantasia*. The clothes danced to the song of the wind, and the moves were always new.

Sometimes the sun was low in the sky before she finished taking in the clothes.

In the all-purpose room known as "Grandma's office," the washtubs waited in a line. Kati had to sort the clothes and place them in the correct tub: Grandma's clothes, Grandpa's clothes, Kati's clothes, each in its own tub. The pillow-slips and sheets, tea towels and table napkins, the cleaning rags— or "yucky cloths" as Grandpa called them— all were separated out, not only as a hygiene measure (an over-the-top hygiene measure, according to Grandpa), but for the convenience of Sadap when she came to do the ironing for Grandma.

Grandma would come in and arrange the tubs in order of priority. Kati's school uniforms took pride of place as these had to be washed, ironed, and worn again within the week.

The sound of the rain hissing and splashing on the roof was greatly improved by the plink-plonk drumming on the tubs that had been left outside. Kati lay and listened with pleasure. But she would begin to get jumpy if the rattle of the rain was drowned out by thunder rumbling from the skies. The sound of lightning strikes seemed always to be echoed by a cry of heart-stopping despair. Was this just the thunder ringing in her ears, or was this a cry coming from somewhere in the darkest recesses of her memory? Kati always wondered. Grandma would open the bedroom door and come to lie down, holding Kati in her arms until they both fell asleep till morning. Kati lay curled up in Grandma's embrace. She didn't want to hear the sky, the rain, the cry, the sound of that woman. Grandma's cool, smooth skin was faintly scented. Grandma never sang her a lullaby or told her a story to calm her agitated spirit, but she stroked Kati's back softly, regularly, rhythmically, sending her to sleep. Once, Kati half-opened her eyes to look up at Grandma and saw her eyes shining. A distant flash of lightning gave just enough light for Kati to see that, in the darkness, Grandma was crying.

4

The Paddleboat

No one ever spoke of Mother.

Grandpa bought a little flat-bottomed boat to paddle in the flooded fields when the rainy season came. He said it was a nice way to escape Grandma's bustle. Kati and Grandpa would go off, just the two of them. They set off in the late morning most Saturdays, Grandpa paddling in a leisurely fashion, passing down the waterway, looking at the fruit trees growing along the banks: mangoes and rose apples mingled with casuarinas that liked to grow by the waterside. Grandpa didn't stop and rest but called greetings to all the people he saw. Uncle Sohn was hauling up his net from the pier in front of his house, and it looked like he had a good catch of *tapean* fish. Grandpa said on the way home he'd stop and get some for Grandma to fry up for Kati's dinner.

The little boat drew away from the deep shade of the waterways and moved toward the open field that seemed to stretch as far and wide as the eye could see. The water in their wake was ruffled by a gentle breeze, and away in the distance the paddy fields glinted bright green. Grandpa let the boat drift in the center of the field and began to pick lily stems. You had to look carefully to make sure that you had the *pun* lilies, not the *peuan* lilies with their dry bitter taste. The *pun* lilies had bright yellow flowers and round leaves with no veins. Their crisp fresh stems were delicious, dipped in the pungent chili sauce that Grandma had wrapped in lily leaves along with newly harvested rice for their lunch. Kati had fun breaking the lily stems up into little pipes and fitting them back together as a necklace. Sometimes she would see a raft of *krajup* growing together. She liked them better than water chestnuts, and Grandpa would gather them in the bottom of the boat to take home to boil and eat. Then there were the water hyacinths, with their fragile, pale purple blooms. If you held them in your hands, in no time at all they would wither away. The white morning glories were pretty too. Grandpa said if you were an artist like Monet, you could make them just as beautiful on canvas.

Grandpa would paddle peacefully, not worrying about what time he left home, where he had to be next, and when he had to be home by. Grandpa said they weren't on a tour according to the dictates of the railway time table. They were on a tour according to the dictates of their own hearts.

The flat-bellied boat with its stubby bows made an excellent conveyance. It did not pollute the environment, but cut through the clear waters to the stroke of the paddler. If you paddled into a flock of pond skaters, the insects would scatter wildly, making mayhem.

Grandpa and Kati didn't need to speak. They let the little boat and the water greet each other instead. The sun seemed far away in the sky, even though its rays were stronger now. But around them the water completely covered the field, acting as a coolant to cut out the heat. Time seemed to stand still. Water and sky, wind and sun framed a picture in the center of which floated the little boat. Nevertheless, a boat can't keep going forward without eventually reaching its destination, no matter how enchanting the journey.

5

The Old Shelter

Kati no longer remembers Mother's face.

The destination Grandpa chose, on the basis of his rumbling stomach, was the little water-side shelter under the big East Indian walnut tree.

This was their usual rest stop on trips to the field, because it was so well placed. The lone walnut tree stood at the edge of the field, its broad canopy left to grow freely and grace-fully, casting a convenient shade over the dilapidated roof of the old shelter. The thick planks of the shelter still held well, though they creaked and squeaked with every step, sounding like an elderly person greeting a long-awaited visitor. The gentle sunshine filtered through the leaves and branches of the walnut tree. Sunlight penetrated a hole in the roof, falling on the raised wooden platform below. Grandpa gave the platform a cursory wipe before spreading out his long cotton scarf, like a picnic rug, for them to sit on. Kati opened the basket Grandma had packed for them: rich sweet chili sauce, crispy fried catfish salad, sweet pork, and salted eggs, which they mixed with rice and finished off, with Grandpa muttering that it was for this he loved Grandma and no other.

They had not even time for their eyelids to grow heavy after the big meal before they heard someone hailing them from across the water. A number of boats were heading toward them. Headman Boon was bringing the villagers to meet with Grandpa. They had not made an appointment, but Grandpa was their counsel in times of trial, and everyone in the district was courteous and considerate to him.

Word spread quickly in the little community as to when Grandpa was out and about, and the old shelter was a convenient meeting place for those who wished to consult him.

Tong was a member of the deputation too. He gestured for Kati to come over to him while the grown-ups talked. But first Kati liked to hear Headman Boon's introductory remarks. He always said the same thing: that the village by the water was indeed lucky that Grandpa had chosen to return from Bangkok and retire to his ancestral home, which at the time had been left completely deserted and had fallen into disrepair; that Grandpa, who had studied abroad and was a first-class lawyer, was well-known throughout his home and, indeed, the entire kingdom; that Grandpa had made a fortune, but had helped so many people; that if it had not been for Grandpa, the villagers would have been exploited, taken advantage of, and the land of their ancestors . . . Here Grandpa raised his hand to stop the flow of words and asked smoothly if they were planning to conduct the *Kwan Narc* recital, that part of the

Buddhist ordination ceremony where the ordinand recalls his debt of gratitude to his mother for conceiving him, bearing him, and delivering him. Grandpa asked if they would like to include the nine months he spent inside *his* mother's womb in their recitation. This raised a shout of laughter that could be heard clear across the water.

Kati slipped away. Behind the shelter, steps led down to the water, and she sat swinging her legs, letting her toes dip into the water. Tong was never able to sit idle, and he had made a toy boat for Kati that floated on water, a bit of coconut husk with leaves stuck in it as a mast and sails. They raced their boats, thrashing the water with their hands to make them go faster. If they went so far from the shelter that not even a long stick could reach them, then Tong would swim for them. He was a good swimmer who could stay underwater for long periods. But if you were comparing Tong to a fish, you'd have a hard time finding one whose white teeth were the first thing you saw as it came out of the water. When they were tired, they sat and rested. Tong liked to ask Kati about stories she was reading or had just read. Tong said he couldn't understand why when he read them himself they were nowhere near as exciting.

It was a long time before the deputation left, and the sun was slowly setting when Kati walked back into the shelter. Grandpa was folding a letter and replacing it in an envelope. His face, when he looked up at Kati, seemed drained and weary, not unlike the old shelter, which had seen sun and rain, seen so much of the world that every fiber of wood was steeped in the past and no longer had any hope for the future.

6

Big Jars, Small Jars
*Kati wanted Mother to pick her up
from school sometimes.*

Kati never tired of reading *The House of Sixty Fathers*. It was the story of a child orphaned in a war in China, and a fat pig whose owner had named it Glory of the Republic. The story ended with the pig and the boy meeting sixty American soldiers. Kati loved this story. Grandpa had read it aloud to her until his voice was hoarse, while he was waiting for Kati to learn to read it herself. And it was because of this book that Kati liked to call her home on the water "The House of Sixteen Jars."

There were almost too many of these big water storage jars. Still, there was a reason behind each one of the sixteen, according to Grandma's hygiene principles. The jars were strictly segregated according to their function: drinking water, washing water, cooking water. No mixing was allowed. Grandpa scratched his head wondering what the difference was. Whether the water went down your throat or washed your feet, it was all the same to him. But Grandma stood her ground. It was not the same. Cooking water went in the big dragon jar in the kitchen. Washing water went in the huge cement jar under the house (quite a spacious area, as the house was the old-fashioned kind built on stilts). As for the jar that held the drinking water, that was the most special. It went under the rain pipe, and the water in it was then boiled, decanted into bottles, and drunk to quench your thirst. Grandpa said that for goodness' sake, there was such a thing as tap water, and why did Grandma have to create more housework for herself? Fortunately, Grandma didn't hear this remark.

Kati's favorite jar was a small ceramic one decorated with dragons. It looked precious, unlike the earthenware ones, which were sold door-to-door from a loaded boat on the waterway. This jar was glazed inside and out. Inside, it was a shade of blue-green Grandpa called "crow's egg green." On the outside was the dragon pattern. Most important, it had a lid, and Grandma used the jar to store rice. When it was filled with rice, it was too heavy for one person to lift.

By the stairs was a little water jar. This was for washing your feet, before you came upstairs from the yard or the underneath part of the house. Along the path to the road there was a big open jar in which Grandpa grew water lilies, raised with his own hands.

Yes, when you counted them all, there were at least sixteen jars. At the end of the rainy season, they washed out the jars that held the drinking water before closing them up, ready to refill the following year. Kati liked to climb inside one of them and feel the cool earthenware against her skin. The biggest jar had plenty of room for her to make herself comfortable, and it made a great hiding place known only to Kati. Consequently, Grandpa never knew that Kati overheard him say to someone on the phone, ". . . so you want to wait till the end of the school term? Do you really think we have that much time?"

7

The Scraping Rabbit

Kati wanted to see Mother carrying the shopping home from market.

"Good timing! I could do with an extra pair of hands right now," Grandma greeted Tong as he entered the kitchen.

Earlier that morning Grandma had made a big pot of pork curry to offer the monks for the meal they took before noon, their last meal for the day. She said it was her New Year offering, even though Grandpa reminded her that, in these parts, people made their big offering at the Songkran water festival in April. Grandma retorted that it wouldn't hurt to make the offering now, just in case they happened to be somewhere else at that time, and anyway, whose business was it when she felt moved to make an offering?

Tong was dutifully returning one of Grandma's cooking pots from the temple. Grandma pointed to the coconut scraper, known to the villagers as a "scraping rabbit," in the corner of the kitchen next to a pile of split coconuts. Tong grasped the scraping rabbit and the basin of coconuts and briskly made his way to the yard area under the house. The shredded coconut would be squeezed and strained for its sweet white coconut milk—called *ka-ti* in Thai—which was an important ingredient in Grandma's pumpkin dessert. Grandma's voice followed him downstairs, calling to him to leave her a couple of coconuts. She would scrape them extra finely herself later to garnish her steamed rice cakes.

Kati had often wondered why the coconut scraper was called a "rabbit." Whichever way she looked at it, the scraper looked nothing like a rabbit with long ears. Finally, she'd decided that the metal plate that did the actual scraping had teeth that stuck out like the buck teeth of a rabbit. Tong was an expert at this task. You could tell from the way he crouched with one knee on the body of the rabbit and the other touching the floor, smiling as he spun the coconut shells with a fluid movement. His white teeth and the teeth of the scraping rabbit gave them something in common.

The evening meal passed quietly in contrast to the bustle of the afternoon. The breeze from the river was so cold it stung your skin as it, too, made a final salute to the passing of the old year. The huge moon beamed down on them, showing off its beauty, and Kati could see a rabbit in the moon quite clearly. The three people on the veranda gazed up at the moon as if spellbound. Grandpa said, quite casually, that wherever people were, they still looked up at the same moon.

Kati knew that Grandpa meant one person in particular was looking up at the moon right now, just as they all were. The one person that Kati's heart yearned for with every breath she took.

8

The Pot-Scourer
Kati wonders if Mother ever thinks of her.

Grandpa called Grandma's pot-scourer his "wish-spurner." Grandma spurned Grandpa's wishes and refused to buy an electric rice cooker. "The world has progressed, you know," Grandpa's voice sounded loudly from the kitchen door, and he stalked out, shaking his head. He muttered to Kati, was it that Grandma was worried that the villagers would not accept her as one of them? Because she should know that all the villagers hereabouts plugged in an electric appliance to cook their rice.

It was clear that Grandma hadn't always been a housewife. Grandpa said it'd taken her only a couple of years to crack the role, and now there was no trace of the personal secretary to the executive director of a five-star hotel that she had once been.

Grandpa felt constantly frustrated by Grandma's making life difficult for herself. Sometimes Kati felt that Grandma was scared of not having enough to do. She always had a project on the go in the kitchen, making sweet desserts to give to the monks when they came in the morning bearing their alms bowls. Grandpa said it wasn't that Grandma was such a great cook, more that she invested in quality ingredients that did the trick.

Kati always had wonderful snacks and sweets to fill up on after school. If she had to do homework or prepare for an exam, she didn't have to lift a finger; Grandma would place the snacks right by her. Or else Grandma would store them in a row of big glass jars for her to choose from, just like in Uncle Chiang's store at the bus stop. Kati wasn't bothered by exams, though she liked to get them out of the way as soon as possible. The holidays looked promising this year, with lots of fun activities. First would be stargazing. Grandpa had given her a telescope and a map of the constellations for the New Year. She hadn't even taken the telescope out of the box yet. And Kati wanted to go to the special camp the school had organized, but she'd have to ask Grandpa's permission when Grandma was in a good mood. If Grandma disagreed with Grandpa, there was a good chance that Kati would miss out on going to camp.

Or then again, maybe Kati would go birdwatching with Tong. Mostly they watched waterbirds or birds that lived on the edges of the fields. Tong carried his sketchbook everywhere, and when he saw a bird he'd sketch it and then compare it later with a reference book to find out what bird it was. Grandpa encouraged him in this, frequently getting him bird books from overseas. Everyone in the house counted Tong as a member of the household, and Kati often suspected that, as well as helping out with the chores, Tong must have done some great favor for Grandma and Grandpa in the past.

The rice was boiling in its pot on the stove. Kati pulled out the pot-scourer to wipe up the rice water that had frothed over. She needed to use it to tilt the pot over on one side so the remaining water would boil away, leaving the rice fluffy and dry. It couldn't be that difficult, she had seen Grandma do it so often.

Just then Grandma hurried into the kitchen. Her gaze swept the room as she complained that she couldn't find the pot-scourer. Kati could only look at her in amazement. Couldn't Grandma see that she was holding it in her own hand instead of complaining that she couldn't find it? When Kati told her where it was, Grandma seemed greatly put out and sent Kati off to set the table.

These days Grandma's thoughts were often elsewhere.

9

The Urn for Incense Sticks
It was only Mother's voice that Kati could remember well.

The shrine room, with its tiers of gold-lacquered tables, was another place Grandma spent a lot of time each day. On the highest tier rested the image of Buddha.

Kati picked jasmine blossoms and threaded them onto thin stalks of bamboo to place in the altar vases. When she'd had her bath and was nice and clean, Kati would take the vases in to Grandma. The shrine room always seemed cool and pleasant. Grandma said it was a blessing from the holy images whose merciful protection extended to everyone in the house. Grandpa muttered that actually it was because the shrine room was on the north side of the house and got all the wind and none of the sun.

Before the shrine was a large urn for incense sticks. Grandma liked to light incense sticks in offering to Buddha. Kati didn't like the heady aroma of the incense, and the smoke stung her eyes and throat. But she liked to see the flames of the candles, burning steadily under their glass shades. Kati would look into the flame for long periods while Grandma was saying her prayers. Line by line, verse by verse, her prayers seemed to go on forever. Grandpa said that if Grandma collected bonus points for all her prayers, there should be enough for a free frequent-flier ticket to heaven for him, too. He'd laughed, enjoying his own joke, but Grandma had been cross with him for days afterward.

The incense urn was filled to the brim with fine white sand. Kati couldn't imagine where Grandma had found such white sand, there was certainly none nearby, as the sand round here was coarse and brown. Kati liked the sensation of pressing the incense sticks into the smooth surface of the sand. Once in a long while, the urn had to be taken outside and emptied and the sand changed. Kati could lift the urn, but couldn't manage to carry it down the stairs. Grandma didn't risk carrying it herself, either; this was a task she found someone to help her with. Sometimes Tong helped. He would also help Grandma pour libations on the Buddha statue, wipe clean the platform that held the Buddha, and generally dust and polish every part of the shrine. Usually this spring cleaning was carried out just before the Songkran water festival.

Wash, clean, and get rid of all the grime that had accumulated over the year, to start afresh, with good fortune, said Grandma.

If people's hearts were like the white sand in the urn that could be emptied and refilled again, all clean and white, how good that would be.

Kati started from her reverie when

Grandma, having knelt and touched her forehead to the ground in homage to Buddha, turned and looked at Kati. Kati would never forget that picture, no matter how much time should pass, the picture of Grandma looking at her, and the sound of Grandma's voice that accompanied the picture.

"Kati, my dear, do you want to go see your mummy?"

PART II

The Home by the Sea

10

Peacock Flowers

*It had been many years since Kati
had seen Mother.*

Red sprays of peacock flowers rushed by on either side, and the car sped forward as if it were flying. Kati felt light and insubstantial, like an empty box. For the past two days her heart had pounded with excitement. It was as though the events that followed Grandma's question had happened to someone else, as though Kati could see herself moving and speaking from the outside. She saw Grandpa walk into the room. He pulled Kati to him and hugged her tightly. He spoke slowly when he told her that Mother was ill, very ill. She had been to many places for treatment, but could not get better.

Mother's friend Aunt Da came to pick up Kati and Grandpa and Grandma. Grandpa had let Kati decide for herself whether she wanted to see Mother or not. Grandpa shook his head when he said that, so far, everyone had made decisions for Kati, but this time it was up to Kati to decide for herself. They left early in the morning. In the car the air was very cool, while outside the sunshine grew fiercer with every passing minute. Aunt Da drove with the practiced ease of one who knew the route well. She slowed the car effortlessly to pause at the tollgates, then accelerated smoothly onto the elevated expressway, which swung round to the right and left like a roller coaster in a fun park. The expressway ran between clustered skyscrapers, and advertising billboards replaced the views of the countryside. It seemed only a few seconds later that the car descended to the freeway that led away from the city. Kati's attention wandered, and she fell asleep, waking to see the red flames of the peacock flowers.

The car headed south. On the left were the sea and the beach; to the right a range of mountains could be seen in the distance. Grandpa and Grandma were talking in soft voices in the backseat. Aunt Da spoke on her mobile phone from time to time, and Kati could tell that there was only a short distance to go before she would see her mother.

Grandpa called peacock flowers the "flame of the forest." Kati had only recently learned that the real name of these trees was the European peacock flower. The Thai species had flowers of many colors—yellow, pink, and red, not just the orangey red she saw now. Kati liked the way the peacock flower trees were planted in an orderly row along the road. Grandpa said there used to be a lot more of them before they built the airport and cut most of them down. When Aunt Da noticed Kati craning her neck to see the trees, she pulled over at a wayside shelter. Grandpa was happy to have the chance to stretch his legs, and Grandma brought along her basket of snacks. The trees seemed different from the

ones Kati had left at home. There was an unfa-
miliar tang in the air too, and Kati guessed it
must be the salty smell of the sea.

The mobile telephone rang again. Although
the ring tone was soft, they all started. Aunt Da
said gently into the phone that they would be
there very soon. It was the first time Kati had
seen ever Grandpa holding Grandma's hand.
Grandma was gripping her basket so tightly
with her other hand that her knuckles were
white. The tips of Aunt Da's fingers were icy
cold where they touched Kati's warm palm. Kati
bent and picked up some of the little sprays of
peacock flowers from where they lay on the
ground nearby. They still had their pretty red-
orange petals. She took them to give to Mother.

The car stopped in front of a small house
that looked clean and white with its contrast-
ing window frames of bright blue. No one
needed to tell Kati what to do; she opened the
car door and let her heart lead the way.

Mother kissed Kati over and over again. Her
long, soft hair smelled sweet and refreshing.

Mother's voice, though hoarser than Kati remembered, was no less loving.

"Hug Mummy tight, Kati, my darling child."

It made no difference that it was Kati hugging Mother, not Mother hugging Kati. Their tears of happiness flowed and mingled together. Kati's arms folded round her mother just as she had dreamed. Her embrace spoke the words of love she could not utter, that she loved Mother with all her heart, that she understood why they had to be apart, that she had missed her so. Kati did not know how long it was before she let go of her mother.

The peacock flowers were in a glass vase by the side of the bed already.

11

Wind Crabs

No one knew how much time
Mother had left.

Kati had always thought that a beach would be made up of smooth, fine, soft sand stretching off into the distance. Only when she saw it for herself did she realize there was more to a beach than that. From the veranda of the house you could see the little pools of water the sea had forgotten and left behind the night before. A horse had left a long trail of hoofprints on the sand, right at the water's edge. The person leading the horse had left footprints too. Grandpa said it was a good

thing that the horse hadn't left them a sou-
venir of a more substantial kind. He said
nowadays people tending horses were armed
with plastic bags, so they could pick up the
smelly dung and put it in the bins the council
had provided at intervals along the beach.

On the sand there were other strange
markings. Kati sat and studied these at length.
It was as if someone had rolled grains of sand
into little balls and scattered them on the
ground in a strange dotty pattern. Mother's
friend Uncle Kunn said it was the work of
wind crabs. As they dug their holes, they threw
out the sand shaped into little balls by their
claws. There must be lots of crabs living on the
beach, but Kati had yet to see if they lived up
to their name and ran as fast as the wind.

Uncle Kunn did not speak much, but it was
as if he had told Kati about all sorts of things and
knew what she was thinking too. Sometimes
they walked in silence along the beach in the
evening. When they were tired, they looked for a
place to rest and often sat together on the sea-
walls of shuttered-up beach houses.

From Uncle Kunn, Kati heard all about this disease with many names. Americans called it ALS, or amyotrophic lateral sclerosis. The English called it MND, or motor neurone disease. The French called it *maladie de Charcot* (after the doctor who had first identified the condition 150 years ago). Uncle Kunn spoke of Lou Gehrig, the American baseball player who'd had this disease and was the first to make its symptoms known to the general public. He went on to explain that there was no cure. Those with the condition became progressively weaker as muscle deteriorated. Eventually they lost control of their muscles, their arms, their legs. It became more difficult to speak, swallow, and eventually breathe. The final result was total paralysis. Kati heard about the spirometer, the BiPAP machine, and many other things that floated past her ears and disappeared with the sea breeze. Aunt Da said Uncle Kunn was a dab hand at writing scripts for radio advertisements. It must have been true, because when Uncle Kunn explained to Kati, who was nine years old, about Mother's illness, complicated things became easy to understand.

The figures Uncle Kunn mentioned were also easy to understand. Males got it more than females. Most people who had it were between forty and seventy. Fifty percent of people died within eighteen months of diagnosis. Only ten percent of people lived longer than ten years. Twenty percent lasted five years.

There was a time when Kati might have found these statistics no more than interesting facts, but that time was past. Mother had first developed symptoms when she was thirty-three. She had been ill for nearly five years now.

The wind crabs scuttled down their holes before her eyes. Uncle Kunn asked casually if Kati would like to run a race with him, if he let her start from the pine tree in front of them, and whoever made it to the hotel first would win. Kati didn't wait to be asked a second time. She set off running.

The wind, mingled with the hot air rising

from the sand, blew in her face. Kati ran faster and faster. She was running to the horizon. Her feet felt the fine sand beneath them in a way that Mother was no longer able to do . . . in a way that Mother had once done. Kati's hands were clenched, and they pumped up and down in rhythm. Her hands were moving in a way that Mother's could no longer move. Kati raised her hand to wipe away her tears. That easy movement was something Mother could no longer do, though Mother had once done so just as easily as Kati.

The hotel entrance flashed by out of the side of Kati's eye, but she couldn't stop. She raced on and prayed that the beach would continue before her, an endless beach. It was only when her knees gave way and she fell onto the sand that Kati realized she was soaked in sweat. Her legs were trembling. She cried without shame, as though all her defenses had been shattered, as she had never cried before. Someone knelt down beside her and gathered her up in a hug. It was a good while before Uncle Kunn spoke. He said that her crying would flood the wind crabs' holes. Kati laughed through her tears. Uncle Kunn shifted and gestured for Kati to hop onto his back. The view to either side looked different from up on high. Uncle Kunn laughed when he said that she probably hadn't been thinking of how they would get back home when she'd run so hard and long.

The sky was dark now. Light shone from the veranda of Seaview Villa. The tide was high so the beach had shrunk, and on the sand no trace remained of the wind crabs.

12

Sea Morning Glories

Everyone knew that Mother had less and less time left with every passing minute.

"Look, Miss Chomcha-da, if you don't get yourself together, it's no use coming to me for sympathy if you lose out on Mr. Right, okay. Just give it a go!"

Uncle Dong's voice sounded from the kitchen. He was Mother's cousin and also a close friend from university days. Everyone had come over to stay in the big house to keep Kati and Grandpa and Grandma company, and to visit with Mother as often as she could see them. The smaller house, where Mother was, was a single-story bungalow closer to the beach. The big house was also painted white with the same bright blue window frames, but it had two stories. The owner had built them as holiday homes but afterward bought a bigger piece of land and built a resort there, keeping this one for his personal use. Aunt Da said the owner owed Mother a big debt of gratitude, as Mother had helped him avoid a court case that would have shut down his business. When he heard that Mother needed a place to rest and take care of her health, he placed the house at her disposal for as long as it suited her. Of course, Mother paid no attention to his protests and asked Aunt Da to pay rent every month.

Aunt Da was pink in the face when Kati and Uncle Kunn came into the kitchen. Uncle Kunn asked who was beating who at what. But instead of answering, Aunt Da pushed past them with an obstinate look on her face. Uncle Dong had to announce loudly that if Uncle Kunn had no better business than to hang round looking handsome, he might as well help Aunt Da set the table for dinner.

Uncle Kunn looked puzzled but went to help as he was told. Kati was puzzled too. If anyone round here was handsome, it was Uncle Dong—he just needed to lose a little weight round his middle and grow a bit more hair.

Uncle Dong was holding a spray of flowers that looked familiar to Kati. The little purple blossoms sprang in profusion from a long creeper tendril, and Kati remembered the sea morning glories that she'd seen growing on the beach beside the front fence. Their leaves were bright green and heart shaped, and they were used to treat jellyfish stings. This time Uncle Dong had picked them not for their medicinal properties but to decorate the dinner table. Uncle Dong had a magic touch when it came to artistic arrangements of any kind. Wherever he placed things they always looked beautiful.

But you can't eat table decorations, as Grandma had remarked when Grandpa tactlessly praised Uncle Dong in front of her. It was as though there was a little battle going between Grandma and Uncle Dong. If Grandma knew Uncle Dong was coming, she would move into the kitchen and excel herself in cooking a fantastic meal. Uncle Dong would then set about finding all sorts of props to create a sumptuous table setting. Decorations could either make the meal taste even better or completely overshadow it according to Uncle Dong. On tonight's table the sea morning glories reigned as the "queen of flowers."

"So how's my lovely Burmese maiden?" Uncle Dong called out to Kati. Grandma, who was just coming in with a serving dish, gave him a furious look. Kati left them to battle it out and went to have her bath and change her clothes before going to see her mother.

She was still asleep. Kati went and sat close by her. Mother's face was calm under the mask with the tube linking it to the BiPAP machine, and Kati thought about what Uncle Kunn had said, that Mother had chosen not to have a tube inserted in her throat even though that would prolong her life, because it would mean that she could not speak. Mother had chosen to reduce the time she had left so she could speak with them till the last. Kati thought of the fairy story about the little mermaid who had chosen to have her tongue cut out so that her tail could be turned into legs to help her find her true love. Kati guessed that Mother no longer had a true love to seek.

That night was especially bright and cheery, as all of them were able to be there together. The longer and more often Mother slept, the more it seemed everyone was dropping in to spend time with her. Aunt Da was with Mother almost all the time. Grandpa said Aunt Da was not only Mother's right hand, but also her left hand and both her feet. Not only that, Grandpa winked at Kati, but Aunt Da also had a good head on her shoulders, and although there were plenty of people with heads on their shoulders, not many actually used them to think. If Aunt Da had to go to Bangkok on business, then Uncle Kunn would immediately come to take her place. Sometimes he must have arrived in the middle of the night, because Kati would wake to find him already sitting on the sofa at the end of Mother's bed, asleep.

The topic of conversation at the table was a

new television game show that was extremely popular. The idea for the show had been Mother's, and everyone knew that its success was due to her hard work negotiating with the overseas producers. Mother had persuaded them all to go shares in the enterprise and had asked Uncle Kunn to be the front man. Tonight everyone at the table raised their glasses to celebrate with Kati, as the profit from the deal would go toward Kati's education. The grown-ups at the table roared with laughter when Kati, mystified, asked, "But I go to the local temple school, why do we need a lot of money for my education?"

The meal was every bit as delicious as the cook had intended. Mother's meal was liquid and was fed to her by a tube directly through her stomach into her intestine, but she joined them at the dining table in a comfortable wheelchair with a nurse by her side. Mother's face beamed with joy, and although she couldn't really laugh, she clearly shared all the fun. Kati sat next to her. She noticed Mother sometimes yawned or made sounds that seemed unconnected to the conversation—a weird symptom of her condition.

The sky had long been dark, but the lights from the little candles Uncle Dong had placed along the veranda swayed and shone, weaving a gentle radiance that soothed the eyes. It was as if the candles wished to compete with the moon, which was full and round in the sky. Its silvery light fell on the water below and was reflected back again with a full heart. Mother turned her face to look at the moon and said that soon she would be up there to watch over Kati for all time.

Kati sat quietly, keeping her mother company. The moon was so beautiful that Kati wished every night could be a full-moon night. Wannee, Mother's nurse, brought in a shawl. Kati rose then and wandered into the pantry, intending to pour herself a drink of water. The scene she saw there was Aunt Da held in Grandma's arms, her whole body shaking with sobs. Tears bathed Uncle Dong's cheeks, while Grandpa and Uncle Kunn stood with their backs turned. Kati saw the fragile purple flowers of the sea morning glory withered on top of the fridge. Someone must have forgotten to put water in the vase.

13

❧

Jellyfish
*Living in the present moment
is no easy matter.*

No clouds could be seen in the wide canopy of the sky. It looked like a seamless cloth of bright blue.

Kati lay on her back and floated in the sea, which was as still as glass. The orange sun had only just popped up over the horizon, so the air was cool and refreshing. Actually, Kati preferred to swim in the late afternoon when the high waves crashed against the shore, one after the other, dashing seawater in your face and eyes. The challenging afternoon waters were more exciting than the calm morning waters, which weren't so different from the canal at home. But Aunt Da didn't like waves, and Mother would not let Kati swim alone. As Kati was a good child, she obediently followed Aunt Da down to the water for her "morning swim," as Grandpa called it, using the English words.

Seen from the sea, the little white house was on a hill, surrounded by a low fence, above a stone breakwater. The little fence offered only token protection, but the stone breakwater was like a fortress, holding back the force of the sea. The walls of the house were whitewashed plaster, like the houses in the Greek isles that Uncle Dong had talked about. On the veranda there was a long bench hanging from chains like a swing, and its lemon yellow cushion added to the cheerful, comfortable atmosphere. This was a house that had never known gloom and despair, incredible as that might seem.

The water came up to Aunt Da's waist. She refused to swim properly, but just splashed and waded around. Aunt Da said you had to look carefully to see if there were any jellyfish around.

Kati liked jellyfish. She wished Tong could see them. She was sure he'd cry out in surprise— they certainly looked nothing like the jellyfish you'd eat in a bowl of seafood noodle soup.

When she came out of the water, Kati hurried to tell her mother how she'd seen the jellyfish floating along with the waves. Mother said she liked to see them too, looking like parachutes in midair. Kati couldn't understand what she meant, so Mother found some photos on the Internet for her. The jellyfish looked very relaxed as they swayed to and fro in the water, their upper parts like mushroom flowers seen from above, furling and unfurling. They really did look like the para-chutes that soldiers used when they jumped out of planes. Mother said she'd like to be a jellyfish drifting around with no particular destination. All her life she'd had clear goals and destinations, even now at the very end of her life.

Mother's computer was voice activated. Uncle Kunn said Mother had prepared audio files for when she could no longer use her hands to work on the computer. She couldn't hold a book to read, so she listened to them on tape. Her friends had sent her audiobooks from far away. Some were children's books, and Mother would call Kati to listen to these. If she had the original, Kati would look at the pictures and read along with the tape. Mother liked the fact that the stories were teaching Kati English at the same time.

But what Mother liked most was to look at the photos in her album with Kati. Almost every photo was of Kati alone, taken by Grandpa, who must have sent photos at regular intervals. Mother would ask Kati to tell her all about them, and Grandpa called these sessions "the behind-the-scenes show."

This photo was Kati's fourth-grade class teacher, Teacher Ratree. "Her husband is a teacher too, Mum, but he was assigned to a school in another province. Teacher Ratree applied to get transferred to join him but it's been years now and they're still apart. The big kids say that's why she's such a grump, she's worried her husband will find a new wife. I think she's got a nice smile but she doesn't smile very much. Some people say it's a good thing she hasn't got any children but other people say if she did then maybe she wouldn't feel so lonely. It's weird, Mum, even during the holidays she comes to school. She never seems to go to visit her husband and no one's ever seen him either."

Kati chattered on. Sometimes Mother would interrupt to ask a question, like why this girl smiled so strangely. "Oh, Pirawan fell over. She fell off the slide and broke her jaw. She's got to have this thing in her mouth now that makes her dribble all the time. The other kids call her 'Miss Duh.' They won't play with her. So I ask Pirawan to come and read stories with me. You can't really chat with her, you see, because she can't talk back."

While putting the photo albums away in the drawer, Kati spied a box hiding at the bottom. Inside was an album Kati had never seen before. Mother seemed reluctant to look at it, and Kati thought she must be getting tired, but then Mother motioned for her to sit on the bed next to her and put the album in her lap.

The first picture was of a baby in its mother's arms. The bold handwriting underneath read, "Na-kamon Podjanawitt, February 14, 1993."

14

Frangipani
The past casts a shadow that can point to the future.

"You were born after midnight, so it was Valentine's Day. Uncle Dong was so happy. I don't know where he found the red roses, but they filled the room to overflowing. I had a big fight with the nurse over it. But it was really so pretty, wherever I looked I could see only roses."

Mother sat quietly as though picturing the little hospital room transformed into a bower of love by Uncle Dong's professional artistry.

"Grandpa gave you the name Na-kamon,

which means 'abiding in love.' Grandpa liked the suffix 'Na.' My name has a 'Na' too. Grandpa wanted us to have names that matched."

Mother's name was Na-patra. Grandpa said it meant "abiding in virtue."

"At that time Grandpa and Grandma hadn't moved to the house on the water. Grandpa was crazy about you, actually everyone was crazy about you. Uncle Dong was over the moon. I'd never known him to pay any attention to children before this, but he was so besotted with you that he actually left his work to come and sit by your crib, and of course, he and Grandma ended up fighting over you. Look at this! The photo of your first haircut when you were a month old. And here's the certificate with your name on it, from your naming ceremony. Grandpa's handwriting was so beautiful, we had it framed."

It seemed as though the day had been a happy one for everyone, even though one person was conspicuously absent from all the photographs, one person who was not even mentioned.

Mother's bedroom looked out over the sea. In the afternoon the sea receded so far you could hardly see it. Grandpa said that if you wanted to swim at this hour, you'd have to call a taxi to get you there. The side walls of the house were big glass windows; through them you could see the big frangipani tree with its yellow and white flowers sending forth their sweet scent. Grandma didn't like the tree at all. She said that in the olden days it was bad luck to have a frangipani near your home. Grandpa muttered that this was a resort, not a home. He would have grafted a branch to take back to plant in the garden of the house on the water, except Grandma would probably explode with indignation.

"I'd just moved back to Bangkok. We were living in a condominium right in the center of the city, just the two of us. I was lucky. Everyone wanted to help look after you. Here, this one's of your first birthday. And here's Aunt Da as well. Aunt Da was a trainee in our office right from when she was a student. When she graduated she came to work for me. You've liked her ever since you first met, so I knew I'd chosen the right person as my assistant."

Kati thought she looked funny almost completely bald. Mother had obviously been worried about her daughter's appearance, as she'd fastened a little bow on a wisp of hair on top of her head, and after that she sported the same little bow in every photo.

Kati found it very entertaining. Mother paused at intervals to draw in a breath from a tube that was connected to her BiPAP machine. ALS made her muscles so weak that in the end they became useless. Not only her leg and arm muscles but, far more dangerously, the muscles in her lungs had stopped working, including the muscles that inflated her chest to take in air. Now the BiPAP machine pumped air into Mother's lungs so she could get all the oxygen she needed. When she was asleep she wore a mask, but in the daytime she could just draw on the tube whenever she had difficulty breathing.

"This snap was taken when we were all on

holiday in Singapore. You were about three years old. I went there to work, so Uncle Dong dragged Kunn along too. Uncle Kunn didn't study law like me, but we were in the same tennis club at college. I was in my third year when Kunn came in his first year. No, Uncle Dong was never a tennis player, but he liked to mix with the tennis crowd and watch the young guys play." Mother laughed. "Someday I'll find you the photo of Uncle Dong and Uncle Kunn and me when we were all students together. Aunt Da saw it—and nearly died laughing!"

Mother had been so happy with life and her friends, and Kati had clearly been loved by all, as the old photos showed.

Kati turned the pages till she came to the middle of the album and was puzzled to find it had been only half-filled. What was even stranger was that the last two photos were of Kati alone in a pose that wasn't funny at all.

"Grandma and Grandpa had moved to the house by the canal by then. I encouraged them to go because Grandpa had already put

off going for long enough—it was nearly a
year since their house had been renovated. I
knew it was your Grandpa's dream to return
to the simple village life after he retired. I
wasn't able to visit them as often as I wanted.
I was busy with my work, which was really
more than I could handle. Everyone was into
e-commerce—you know, selling goods over
the Internet. I'd been onto it ever since I was
stationed in Hong Kong, and there was no one
I could really hand it over to. I had to solve all
these problems that came up and advise the
foreign companies setting up in Thailand on
the legal side of things."

Of course, Mother had to stop from time
to time. Her voice became thick, but her eyes
were bright with determination to go on with
her story.

"Then I began to get sick. At first I thought
I'd been working too hard, not resting
enough. I kept dropping things. I'd miss a step
and fall down stairs. I did that both at work
and at home. This picture was taken after I
dropped you coming down from a pedestrian

bridge—we were both a mess, covered with grazes and cuts."

There were grazes on Kati's chubby cheeks, painted red with antiseptic. It didn't seem to have bothered little Kati much, because she was smiling away at the camera, but the photographer must have been mightily shaken by the episode. Even now Mother's voice sounded shaky with emotion. Kati wondered whether Mother should be talking about this when it upset her so. Mother took a long pause before continuing.

"You were hurt because of me so many times—you got lumps on your head, a split lip. You used to cry so loudly when you were hurt, too. But the next minute you would be playing happily as if nothing had ever happened. It was just as I had prayed when I was pregnant with you, that you would always have joy in your heart, whatever happened in your life.

"But at this stage I became more and more certain that something was wrong with me. When I was finally diagnosed, I just couldn't think how I was going to manage my life at all.

I took leave from work and went to live with Grandpa and Grandma. It was then that it happened."

Kati wasn't sure whether she should stay on her own with her mother or go and get the nurse. Mother had said that she wanted to spend as much time as possible with Kati alone, and that if she wanted anything, she could ask Kati to go and get it, but now her face looked so pale, and she was using the BiPAP more and more frequently.

"At some level I guess I was denying to myself that anything had changed. I took you for a ride in the boat to see the sights. Grandpa and Grandma didn't see me go. I'm sure they would have forbidden me to go if they had. 'Course maybe I wouldn't have listened to them either. I wanted to take you to see the big East Indian walnut tree that grows on the edge of the paddy fields. We got to the little shelter there safely enough. You loved the water, the boat, the shelter, the morning glories. We were having such fun playing together that I didn't notice the clouds gathering on the horizon.

"I made my second bad decision. We could have waited out the rain in the shelter and then headed home. But I could see the roof was in pretty bad shape, and I was worried it wouldn't keep the rain out. When I looked again, the rain clouds still seemed a long way off, so I thought I had time to row us back out of the fields. And if we didn't make it home before the rain, we could stop and take cover in the first house we came to on the canal."

Mother lay still for a while. She drew air from the tube again and again.

"I hastily packed up our basket and put on your hat, took your hand, and led you down the steps. The wind was getting stronger and stronger. The boat wouldn't stay still. It was rocking back and forth, knocking against the step. I put you in the boat and turned to undo the rope that moored us to the pier. But my hands . . . the more I tried to hurry, the clumsier I became. I climbed back out of the boat to undo the rope more easily. Finally free from its mooring, the rope slipped from my hands too.

I grabbed the oar, hoping to catch hold of the boat with it. My timing was totally wrong. Even easy things I could no longer do. And the boat just floated away from the pier, bobbing up and down on the waves, the boat in which you were still sitting, completely alone."

Kati could picture the vast expanse of the flooded fields, churned to a wild sea by the storm winds. The sky would not have been bright and clear as it was when she and Grandpa went for their picnic. The heavy clouds would have darkened the whole sky. Thunder would have rumbled over the water, mingling with the roar of the wind and Mother's cries.

"I tried to control my anguish—I called for you to sit still. I was worried you would take fright and try to come to me and the boat would capsize. I knew that I was no longer capable of doing many things. I could not jump into the water and pick you up. I had tried so hard to catch the boat with the oar, but had only managed to tap the side of the boat. My arms did not have the strength to drag a boat against the wind and the water. And the oar now fell from my grasp into the water as well.

"I was like a madwoman. The rain was pouring from the heavens as though the sky had sprung a leak. My voice had to compete with the thunder as I shouted at you to sit still. I really did not know what to do. I cried harder than the sky. I was furious with myself and furious at the rain. But more than anything I was so terrified that it seemed as if my heart had stopped. In utter desperation I cried, 'Please, someone help me. Please help my child.' I screamed at the top of my voice, even though I knew no one could hear me amid the noise of the storm."

Mother should definitely stop talking. Her voice was husky, and she was almost gasping for breath, but something in her eyes told Kati that nothing and no one could stop her.

"And in my heart I prayed every prayer that Grandma had ever taught me, all the ones I could think of. I recited the mantras and I added prayers of my own. You could say I made a promise to all things sacred that if there were such things as miracles, please keep my daughter safe and I would give up everything I owned, everything. Most people say they would give their lives in exchange, but I, of course, had very little life left to give. The sky split with lightning as if acknowledging my promise: If my child was safe, then I would never so much as touch her again. I would go far away from my child and never bring her into danger again."

Tears streaming down her cheeks, Mother sobbed until she collapsed in a heap. Kati took Mother's hand and kissed it, held it against her cheek. She lifted her mother's arm so that she was embracing Kati. Kati hugged her mother tight. Mother's face pressed against Kati. Her flesh felt cold as ice. Kati whispered that she was here, here with Mother, that they two would never be separated again.

The frangipani blossom had fallen on the ground below the window, as if it could no longer bear the suffering of these two hearts.

15

Sand Flies
At journey's end

Kati liked to sit at the edge of the water, making sand castles with Uncle Kunn. What she didn't like were the horrible sand flies that bit you when you weren't aware of them. These tiny creatures had a powerful bite. They would hide in the sand, waiting for their prey, and you wouldn't even know you'd been bitten till you saw the angry red spots at bathtime. The more you scratched them, the itchier they became. Uncle Dong said the bites of the sand flies were like love, an itch you couldn't scratch away and couldn't forget, an itch you were constantly aware of.

Kati used both hands to dig a hole in the sand. When the waves came in, it became a pool, but sand came tumbling in with the water. Soon her deep pool became a shallow pool, and she had to dig it out all over again. But this was satisfying, too, keeping Kati's hands busy while her mind kept returning to the story Mother had told her that afternoon.

So the knight in shining armor who had saved little Kati's life was none other than Tong of the Siamese smile. Mother said that Tong had been quite excited over the arrival of the four-year-old "city girl." He would paddle his boat over to play with her often. That day he had come over to the house in search of his playmate and had followed them to the old walnut tree. His boat appeared just after an enormous lightning strike. Tong was as strong a swimmer as any of the children whose homes were by the water. So it was no great task for him to jump into the water and pull the boat in which Kati sat back to the pier and safety. He had picked Kati out of the boat and placed her right in Mother's lap.

"Like a mother cat with a kitten," said Mother, smiling through her tears at the picture they'd made: Tong, skinny and small for his age, bearing Kati, who was round and chubby. Mother had hugged Kati close, and Tong too. She had been crying and laughing at the same time, there in the middle of the pouring rain, before they climbed the steps to take cover in the little shelter.

Before long Grandpa and other men from the community had braved the storm in their boats to come looking for them, calling for Mother and Kati. They brought blankets and umbrellas, but Mother, Tong, and Kati were already soaked to the bone. That night Kati took ill with a fever. The family had to sit up with her all night, bathing her with damp cloths. It was nearly dawn before her fever abated. As the morning light broke, Mother packed her bags and left the little house on the water without saying good-bye, never to return.

Kati could imagine Grandma's reaction— how distressed she must have been. Kati could also imagine Grandpa's face as he said through set lips that "Pat" must've had her reasons to act in this way, and that some day she would tell them why. From that time on, Grandpa had taken responsibility for caring for Kati.

Kati felt something now biting away at her heart. She stopped digging her hole in the sand and turned to Uncle Kunn.

"Can I use your mobile phone?" she asked.

The morning they had left the house on the water, Tong had handed Kati a scrap of paper and said with a smile that it was the mobile phone number of his uncle, the abbot, in case Kati needed to talk to him about anything. Tong said to ring anytime, because he was the one who took the calls.

Tong's voice, so familiar and so very pleased to hear from her, soothed the ache in Kati's heart in an instant. She saw Uncle Kunn suppress a laugh when he heard Kati's question: "Tong, it's Kati here. Hey, do you want to hear the sound of the sea?"

16

Sea Pines
*It was hard to believe that tomorrow
the sun would rise as usual.*

Mother had been running a temperature for a
number of days now. Dr. Pradit's face was
always serious when he left Seaview Villa.
Aunt Da said that the doctor wanted Mother
to rest up in the hospital, whether the local
one in Hua Hin or one of the big city hospitals
back in Bangkok.

"Even an elephant from Chopstick Mountain
couldn't drag her away from here," said Uncle
Dong, and his voice was shrill.

The day before, Uncle Dong had taken

Kati to Chopstick Mountain. They'd admired the view from the top, where you could look down and see the little white house off in the distance. At the foot of the mountain, you could have a ride on an elephant. Uncle Dong had complained high and low that having elephants at the seaside was totally inappropriate and out of place. There were only a few customers lining up for rides. They were all foreign tourists.

"The mahouts are probably planning to drag them off to the forest and rob them, I shouldn't wonder," said Uncle Dong.

Uncle Kunn whispered to Kati that it was just as well Uncle Dong didn't work in the tourist industry or he'd have lost the country billions with his mistrust of small business. Uncle Dong must have caught something of this, because he went on for some time about how they could hardly be called *small* businesses when elephants were involved.

The thing Mother most wanted to avoid was being on a respirator, a machine that would do her breathing for her. Her gaze was strong and determined when she said this, and those who loved her could only agree. Mother said she was lucky that she could choose for herself the way in which she would die, and she chose to speak until the very end. People couldn't choose to be born and couldn't choose to die, but she asked for the right to make the most of the last opportunities life afforded her. She asked them not to obstruct her in this wish.

Kati had seen them all clustered together many times, discussing Mother's condition. This time they sounded serious when it came to the ways and means to grant Mother's wish. With all of the problems facing them everyone seemed to feel the same restlessness, an urge to get out of the house. They organized a mobile meeting, using the excuse that they had to take Kati out for a drive. Grandma said she'd stay and watch over Mother herself. Grandpa said that was just as well, as he was bound to disagree with whatever she might suggest. Grandma flicked him a glance and said that it was a waste of time to argue with a hotshot lawyer anyway.

The drive ended in a grove of sea pines. The trees stood tall and sturdy, their straight trunks and broad growth giving deep shade. Grandpa said they were a good windbreak because they bent with the wind instead of resisting it. Even the mightiest storm could not break them.

Now it seemed that the meeting had failed to reach any resolution. Uncle Dong said it might as well be group therapy for the grieving. The future was blazingly clear. Mother was like a candle whose light had begun to flicker and fade.

That night Kati woke in the middle of the night. She felt something peculiar in her heart, and thought of Mother's words to her when they were sitting watching the sunset together. Mother had said she didn't want the sky to grow dark.

Kati tiptoed down the stairs to the little house. Uncle Kunn was sitting beside Mother's bed. He was the one person Kati had never seen expressing grief or shedding tears, but in the dim light of the sickroom Kati could see his shoulders shaking with sobs. Finally Kati saw Uncle Kunn throw himself down beside Mother and stay like that for a long time.

There was no movement or flicker of recognition from the face on which the BiPAP mask rested.

Only the thinnest crescent of a moon was left in the sky. The shadows of the sea pines along the fence swayed with the breeze. Time seemed to stand still. It stayed that way till the sun rose in the sky once more, bright and beautiful above the rim of the sea, awakening all creatures on Earth. All except for Mother, who would never waken again.

17

Cicadas
Grief beyond tears

Mother was in a coma for three days before she left them, peacefully. Aunt Da was the first to emerge from the room. She held Kati in a tight embrace. There was no need to speak. She shed no tears that you could see. Her eyes were dry, and she looked as if she had changed overnight.

Mother had donated her body to the hospital, so the funeral rites were only three days long. Grandpa chose a temple on the mountain that had a spacious worship hall. It was an open structure with overhanging caves, a polished wooden floor, and no walls or furniture. At one end was the main Buddha image, and chairs were set out in rows for guests. Uncle Dong was the host for the funeral ceremonies. In the evening guests arrived, one after the other, to pay their respects: colleagues, student-friends, and even clients. Grandpa was concerned for the guests who'd had to travel such a long way to get there. But they were glad to come and make their last farewells to Mother.

The steps to the hall stretched away up the hill. Uncle Dong had set up white poles at intervals, decorated with colorful bouquets of flowers, and had placed little candlelit lamps on each step. The scent of the flowers, the night breeze, and the candlelight created an atmosphere far from sorrowful. Uncle Dong said that Mother had left instructions to do all this, for she wanted them to come together and remember past times together in peace and quiet.

The worship hall was decorated with

swaths of ivory-colored cloth and bright flowers. Kati liked the framed photo on the stand the most: Mother looked so lively, as if she were enjoying being there to look after her guests. She must have escaped the prison that her body had become, and now her spirit was free to go anywhere she liked, wherever her heart desired. Kati was quite certain that one place Mother's spirit would want to be was right beside her.

Aunt Da had gathered her hair into a tiny bun; the bangles that always covered her lower arm had disappeared, and all that was left were her tiny pearl earrings. Aunt Da's clothes were usually an entertainment in themselves. She was fond of draping herself with scarves and pieces of cloth, and whatever she put on looked attractive. The black clothes she now wore made her look unusually thin and pale. Kati saw Uncle Kunn's gaze rest on her with concern as he looked over to where she was greeting the funeral guests and taking care of their drinks and snacks, as well as the offerings they had brought for the monks.

Uncle Kunn had been sticking to Kati like her own shadow. The two of them had no particular tasks in organizing the funeral ceremonies, so, hand in hand, they slipped away to sit outside on the stone benches under a trellis arch of bougainvillea. They listened to the symphony of sounds around them. It seemed the lead part was taken by cicadas, and their constant chorus managed to achieve a certain harmony with the heavy night air, creating an atmosphere that Kati felt privileged to be part of. Normally she would never have been allowed to sit out so late.

By the time the last guests made their farewells and departed, the little lamps had burned very low. Uncle Dong took Grandpa and Grandma home to the beach house. Grandma's stillness made Kati wary of approaching her, and Grandpa exchanged glances with Kati. He wanted her to know that Grandma needed all his attention just now and that it would help if Kati came home later with Uncle Kunn and Aunt Da.

Aunt Da knelt and bowed low to the floor

before the Buddha. She sat before the big framed photograph of Mother for such a long time that Uncle Kunn motioned to Kati to go and sit beside her. Kati met Mother's eyes in the picture, and it seemed that she understood very well what Mother wanted from her.

Kati led Aunt Da by the hand out of the temple hall along with Uncle Kunn. The three of them walked quietly down the steps. Kati was holding Aunt Da's hand on one side and Uncle Kunn's hand on the other. She placed Aunt Da's hand in Uncle Kunn's strong grip. Surely strength and warmth would flow from his big hand into her little thin one. For an instant Kati saw the color that had faded from Aunt Da's cheeks appear again. Mother would have been pleased with the picture they made, a picture whose soundtrack was the chirping of the cicadas in the night.

18

Leadwort
Life . . . goes on.

Tong came with his uncle in time for the last day of the chanting. They'd brought a lot of luggage, and the abbot said they would be leaving for the airport from the funeral. His followers had invited him to travel all the way to America as their guest. So the abbot thought he would take Tong along too to see the world and maybe find a way for him to complete his studies there as well.

"I won't go there to study now," Tong told Kati as he gave her the address of the temple where he and his uncle would be staying. "I'd rather sit the scholarship exam after I finish Year Twelve."

That was several years away. Kati knew Tong's dream was to have a business card that read SUWAN (TONG) WINAIDEE PHD. Uncle Dong said that if Tong could make that dream come true, he was a white elephant with black tusks, a rare beast indeed.

Mother had said we needed a dream to try to make each day better than the last. Kati couldn't think what her dream was, but today was a better day since Tong was here at the seaside with her, even though she had just lost the person she loved the most.

The leadwort blossomed over the fence. You could see the blooms, mauve against the clean white palings. Uncle Dong said there was a spell you could say to make them blossom on demand, but his magic must have lost its power, because Mother never saw the leadwort flowering as she had wanted. The showy blossoms had appeared the very day that Mother had left them all. Uncle Dong blamed the rain. Usually the leadwort flowered thirty days after pruning, but the rain had delayed the flowers, and Mother had missed out on its floral beauty.

Kati sat and admired the flowers in Mother's stead. There were many things in life that Kati didn't understand. Death was one of them. Tong said you had to find comfort in Buddha's teaching, and when Kati was older she would understand it all for herself. To understand all this she'd have to be a lot older than he was now, he concluded with a lame smile.

The goods in the house were gradually being packed up and stored in boxes. Nurse Wannee would go back to Bangkok tomorrow with Tong and his abbot uncle. Uncle Dong would take Grandpa and Grandma home to the house on the water and then meet up with Kati in Mother's home in the city.

As for Kati, she would journey on to find the missing piece in the puzzle of her life.

PART III

The Home in the City

19

The Key Ring
*I knew that some day you
would come here.*

It was close to noon when the car turned into a laneway that broke off from the busy main road. In an instant the heavy traffic receded into the distance. Big East Indian walnut trees grew at intervals along the lane, and to the right ran a little canal. It was nothing like the home by the sea that Kati had left, and vastly different from the home by the water to which she had not yet returned. Yet somehow, the home in the city captured Kati's attention from the instant she first set foot in it.

The entrance hall was floored with marble. The noise from Aunt Da's high heels echoed in the silence as Kati followed her across the foyer. They took a lift to the thirteenth floor, and Uncle Kunn turned to tell Kati that Mother had liked the number thirteen.

"When she was looking for an apartment, she was very pleased to find this one on the thirteenth floor," he said.

"Patra said she wanted Kati to be the one who opened the door," Kati heard Aunt Da whisper to Uncle Kunn. Uncle Kunn bit his lip before handing Kati a key ring in the shape of a red star.

It seemed that Mother had sketched out every detail of what would happen after she left them. It made Kati feel as if Mother was still close by, and helped to ease the dreadful emptiness she felt in her chest.

The olive green door opened with a strong push from Kati. How long had passed, she wondered, since Mother had been strong enough to open this door by herself?

The polished parquet floor complemented the cream-colored walls. The comfortable sofa with its pattern of tiny green, yellow, and white flowers added to the cozy atmosphere. Everything in the room had been designed to fit together beautifully, reflecting the personality of the departed owner. Kati still held the key ring, and now she unlocked one room after another. It was as though she were opening doors to the past, the past that she wanted so much to know.

There was one big bedroom, and a quick glance was enough to tell Kati it had been Mother's room. Next to it were two small bedrooms. One had belonged to a child; this must have been Kati's own room. Another was perhaps a guest bedroom, as it was rather sparsely furnished. Kati guessed it had been used for a nurse like Wannee.

Finally, there was a set of stairs leading up to the floor above. But here Aunt Da pulled Kati back, shaking her head. "Better leave that till later."

The kitchen had big windows, which were an invitation to look down onto the luxuriant trees that grew in a garden below. Uncle Kunn said the garden belonged to an ambassador's residence, and sometimes at night there were parties: The house was decorated with lights and the pretty music wafted up to the thirteenth floor. Kati saw lots of birds she'd never seen before—Tong would have loved to see them and learn what kinds of birds would come to live in the middle of a city.

Kati sat on a tall stool in front of a counter while Aunt Da heated up some food they had bought along the way. Uncle Kunn took plates, spoons, and forks down from the cupboards. It seemed that Aunt Da and Uncle Kunn knew the apartment very well. Kati noticed Aunt Da had tears in her eyes, and her nose was red. Clearly, this whole place spoke to them of Mother. Many objects in the apartment seemed strangely familiar to Kati: memories hidden away in the deepest recesses of her mind, only now being awoken from their long slumber.

On the key ring was one key that Kati had not yet used. It must belong to the room upstairs, the room that Aunt Da did not want her to see just yet. Something awaited Kati on the other side of that last door.

This afternoon Kati would find out what that something was.

20

❧

The Drawers

*You became my future as my own
life began its countdown.*

The room upstairs was in complete darkness
until Uncle Dong drew back the heavy cur-
tains to let the daylight in. Kati squinted in the
light and found herself standing in a room half
the size of the one downstairs. A big cream-
colored desk dominated the room, with a
leather upholstered chair placed behind it.
The chair looked so inviting that Kati sat herself down, while Uncle Dong stood beside her,
his arms crossed, looking out the window on
the scene below. From here you could see the

whole swimming pool, and Kati remembered that Uncle Kunn had said that whenever Kati felt like a swim she had just to say the word.

But for now Kati sensed that this particular moment belonged to Uncle Dong.

When Uncle Dong's face turned to Kati's, he looked strange. Gone was all trace of teasing or merriment. He stood in a formal pose with one hand held out to the right. On another occasion, Kati might have said he looked like a guide taking her round a museum. Kati had been on a school excursion to *Wimarnmek*, the Teak Mansion, and it had made her feel the same way she felt now. Except in this museum she was the only visitor.

"Your mother arranged this room just after she began to get ill. Before that she used it as an ordinary office. You probably won't be able to see it all in a day, starting from that corner over there . . ."

Kati turned to look where Uncle Dong's hand was pointing. There was a long cabinet that took up the entire wall, divided into little drawers, shelves, and glass-fronted display cases.

"Your mother wanted you to know her as well as you possibly could. If you don't count your grandpa and grandma, I'm probably the person who knew her the longest time. So she chose me to bring you here."

His voice was huskier than usual. Kati had almost forgotten that Uncle Dong was actually related to Mother. Uncle Dong's mother and Grandma had been cousins, but Uncle Dong became friends with Mother only when they were both at the same university.

"Some people prepare a memorial book for their own funeral, so those they leave behind will have something to remember them by. Your mother arranged this room especially for you. She gathered together everything that would speak to you of her life. Anything you want to know about your mother, you'll find here."

Kati wanted to know every minute of Mother's life. Although, deep in her heart, she knew there was one period in which she was particularly interested.

Every drawer was numbered with a year.

Mother was born in 1965 right here in Bangkok. The first row of drawers held her childhood. Kati opened the drawers and found neat stacks of albums. Another drawer held notebooks with her school reports, certificates, prize medallions for English, and even handicraft work, carefully placed in plastic folders. A folder containing a knitted woolly scarf bore a label in big letters saying that Grandma had knitted it for her to hand in to her teacher. The label of a smaller packet told Kati that this was Mother's own handiwork that she'd had to knit in class when the teacher's eyes were upon her, but it hadn't been good enough for marking.

Kati looked up at Uncle Dong, who was sitting on the pretty carpet not far from the cabinet.

"That's your mother's own handwriting; the later packets are mine or Kunn's or Da's. She tape-recorded some messages, too. But no videos. Kunn wanted to film your mother, but she wouldn't let him."

If Grandma had seen these, she would have wept buckets. The day before, she'd been folding away some of Mother's rugs and coverlets, and that had distressed her greatly. Grandpa had said you didn't need to go and see sad movies anymore, you could stay home and watch Grandma instead.

Kati continued on to Mother's university years. When she finished her BA, Mother had sat for the Thai bar exam before going overseas. Mother had gone on to get two more degrees from two universities in England. Kati felt as though she were putting together a jigsaw puzzle, but one piece seemed to be still missing.

She did not notice exactly when Uncle Dong got up off the floor, but now he picked up Kati and carried her over to the rocking chair by the window.

"There's something I want to tell you, so let's leave the drawers for a while, shall we?"

21

The Suitcase

You were my one true love.

"That year I went to the flower show in Holland, as I do every year. Your mother rang me—she was really keen for me to have a stopover in London. At that stage your mother had started work as an apprenticed law clerk. She was renting an apartment with a European friend who was an air hostess, and she was always away on flights. Your mother said I could come and stay with her. She promised to take me to see all the sights, but there was something about the sparkle in her voice that made me think she wanted me to see more than just sights.

"And it was so. Your mother came to pick me up at the airport. She was laughing and happy all through the journey on the underground train. My backside hadn't touched down on the sofa before she was telling me that she had something she wanted me to see, a picture of this male friend she was spending time with. I thought to myself, this must be serious, because your mother had never been particularly interested in anyone. She was fond of saying that men didn't go for girls like her. She maintained that men didn't like girls who were sure of themselves and knew what they wanted in life."

Kati must have looked puzzled at this, because Uncle Dong laughed and said that if Mother was right, Kati should keep that uncertain look permanently, so that when she grew up she wouldn't be lonely.

"At first I thought he must be Thai, but your mother said no, he was from one of our neighboring countries but had grown up in

England. Actually, he was even more handsome than he appeared in the photographs. 'Ti, if you want to have a look, go and fetch me the album from the third drawer down."

This drawer was labeled with the year, along with an English name that Kati thought was the law firm where Mother had been doing her apprenticeship that year.

Mother was smiling beside a tall, dark-eyed, dark-haired man. Kati felt a bit odd, looking at the photo of this man. She knew right away who he was. Even a quick glance could tell that his eyes were exactly like hers. Her heart skipped a beat. She quickly turned her gaze to Mother's clothes. She heard Uncle Dong say they had gone to a performance of *Carmen* at Hampton Court. It had been very grand. The whole palace was decorated with white lilies. It was a charity performance, which meant you could take pleasure from helping a good cause and enjoy yourself at the same time. Mother wore a black dress that was fashionably off the shoulder. Her hair was gathered up to show off her elegant neck, and the tiny diamonds in her ears shone no more brilliantly than her eyes.

Anthony Summer was a Webmaster. He'd known Mother from when she'd started working in Internet law. Uncle Dong said he could never forget how happy Mother had been, so he wasn't at all surprised when they announced their engagement. In fact, Uncle Dong thought they might have run off and gotten married even earlier had it not been for the fact that her work took Mother to Hong Kong at that stage.

"I believe that there is a special time for everything in our life, Kati. Your mother rang to ask my advice on whether or not she should go to Hong Kong. She was a very organized person, so she only wanted someone with whom to share her plans. I said, oh yes, and sure thing, but one thing I did say was that true love would last the distance, and that if their love couldn't pass this little test, then it wasn't true love but a fake, and it would be better for her if she knew this right away. I went and met up with your mother in Hong Kong too. It was a lot closer than

London. At one glance I could tell that your mother had made the right decision in coming. Her boss had given her a great opportunity, and she could expect a very bright future. We had a great time in Hong Kong."

Uncle Dong was silent for a long time, as he recalled those happy times when their future stretched long before them.

All at once it seemed that Uncle Dong had thought of something important. He got up and went to a sideboard opposite them, one shelf of which was crammed with books. Kati had just noticed that there was a storage cupboard attached to it as well, and Uncle Dong opened the cupboard door and took something out.

"Here, Kati—this suitcase was your mother's favorite traveling bag. It's so compact, isn't it? At that stage your mother was like a *kinnaree*—the mythological creature that is half bird, half woman. She was flying off all over the place. She went to nearly every country in Asia. I helped her buy the bag, and it really gave your mother value for the money."

Kati listened with her ears as her eyes studied the photos in the album on her lap. There was a photo of them exchanging rings, then of a ceremony in a church, Mother in a white wedding gown beside Grandpa and Grandma. Kati couldn't imagine what Grandpa and Grandma must have thought about their only child marrying so far away from home, not to mention the fact that the girl from Ayutthaya was marrying a boy from Mandalay, cities that in the past had feuded and fought for centuries.

"Sometimes destiny plays such strange tricks on us humans, little 'Ti."

Kati lifted her head from the album.

"It was in this very bag that your Mother carried with her all that she possessed on the day she decided to return to Thailand. Oh . . . all, that is, apart from you, the baby she was carrying in her womb."

22

The Mirror
You were the answer to my prayers.

Kati could not imagine what made two people decide to be together or what made them decide to break up.

She met her own eyes in the big mirror in Mother's bedroom. Tonight Aunt Da and Kati would sleep in this room, and Uncle Dong would sleep in the guest room. As for Uncle Kunn, he had already claimed the sofa in the living room. The reflection in the mirror before her receded, giving way to images from the album that Kati had viewed that afternoon.

The honeymoon in the Lake District, the summer in Scotland, a scenic spot in Hong Kong: It seemed Mother had been as happy as could be. The person next to her looked just as content—or was he? Even then, deep in his heart, could Father have known that Mother was not the life companion he had sought?

"Some people run after dreams their whole lives without realizing that the fulfillment of their dreams is close at hand," Uncle Dong had said, as, hand in hand, he and Kati strolled around the garden.

Earlier that evening Uncle Kunn had suggested they walk to a nearby hotel for dinner. "It'll be a change for you, and I won't have to do the washing-up, what do you say, Kati?" Everyone had agreed, and in only five minutes they passed the guardhouse at the driveway to the hotel. Uncle Dong gestured to Uncle Kunn and Aunt Da to go ahead and book a table, saying he'd take Kati for a walk to look at the garden and work up her appetite. As they retreated, Uncle Dong said nonchalantly, "Do them good to have a little time alone. . . . My goodness, what had to happen before those two got together, with one so cautious and the other not able to see what was going on right before his eyes!"

Kati wasn't paying attention; she was too busy craning her neck to study the jungle around her. The tree in front of her was flowering high above her head, huge yellow flowers with many-layered petals. Uncle Dong said it was a torchwood flower. Kati's neck grew tired, so she lowered her gaze and saw fallen flowers on the ground before her. She gathered them up. They appeared quite fresh. Uncle Dong said he knew the gardener here because he'd been asked to do their flower arrangements on numerous occasions. He would ask permission for Kati to take the flowers home so she could float them in a glass bowl and see how pretty they looked.

Kati had never been to a buffet meal in a restaurant before. There seemed to be a huge amount of food, food to delight the eye and gladden the heart. Aunt Da took her round to read the labels and lifted the lids of the warming dishes, kept steaming hot by the little alco-hol lamps burning beneath them. Kati stood on tiptoe trying to see everything. Some she could see and some she couldn't. In the end Uncle Kunn lifted her up so she could get a better look. Behind her, Uncle Dong was urging her to fill a plate with whatever she fancied, and then on another to put everything she wanted to taste—she shouldn't mix them up. Then when she knew what she liked, she could go back for another helping. Kati blinked: Something as easy as this Uncle Dong had to complicate! She pointed, Aunt Da served the food onto her plate, and in an instant it was done. Uncle Kunn lifted Kati onto her chair before spread-ing her table napkin on her lap. Just the pres-ence of all this lovely food seemed to make life instantly better.

That night, in front of the mirror, Kati picked up a brush and began brushing her hair dreamily. She stared at her reflection in the mirror as the pictures in her head from the evening's events receded. Now Kati knew where her big eyes came from.

She missed her mother so much. Mother must have studied her own reflection in that mirror on countless occasions. Kati thought that images from the past must have popped into Mother's mind too. But Kati had no idea how Mother felt about that past of hers. Was she regretful, angry and vengeful, or tearful and sad? Kati wished she had a magic spell to make the mirror answer her question:

"Mirror, mirror on the wall, tell me how did Mother go on living after losing the love of her life?"

23

Colored Pencils
Love comes in many shapes and colors.

The department store was cool and seemed to spread for miles. Aunt Da walked here from their home in the center of the city. Goods of all kinds were displayed temptingly, inviting them to stop and shop. Kati was content to window-shop until she heard someone call a greeting to Aunt Da.

"Da! Great to see you!"

A woman about the same age as Mother, holding the hand of a child about the same age as Kati, came hurrying over to them. She began to greet Aunt Da vigorously, grasping her by the arm and clasping her hand. She caught sight of Kati and asked in a loud voice, "Is that Pat's daughter? What a sweetie! Last time I saw her she was this big!" The speaker gestured with her hand to indicate the height of the child she'd met. Kati could not have been more than three at that stage.

By the tone of their voices, their questions and answers, it seemed their conversation would continue for some time. The little girl, whose mother called her Pinkie, began to get bored and restless, calling "Mama" and pulling her toward their destination. Kati thought she might like Pinkie. She smiled at her, and Pinkie stopped pulling away and somehow the expression on her face became a little less sour.

"Quite right, let's invite Kati along, shall we? There's an art corner upstairs where kids can make things. Would you like to come too?"

Aunt Da turned to look at Kati. She must have been thinking how nice it would be for

Kati to spend some time with someone her own age.

Kati chose to make a necklace out of beads, while Pinkie did a drawing with colored pencils. The art corner staff was happy to supervise the children, so the adults departed to sip coffee and chat, promising to come and pick them up in an hour.

"If you don't want to stay that long, just tell me, okay? I've got a mobile. I can ask Mama to come and get us, see?" and Pinkie picked up an attractive mobile phone to show off to Kati.

Kati concentrated on the plastic thread on her palm and the little tray full of multi-colored beads. She planned to thread her beads into a long necklace for Uncle Dong to wrap around a vase of flowers. That would make an original and striking table decoration! If she had time, she'd make a smart necklace for Aunt Da to wear with the Mexican patterned blouse she'd just bought.

Kati was engrossed in her task, so she got a shock when she looked over at Pinkie's work of art. It should have been called a work of mess—there were heavy black pencil marks and smeared all over it, as though the artist had drawn something and then changed her mind, scribbling over it in black. Her picture was of two men, a big one and a little one, holding hands. In the distance was a little house engulfed in flames. From the artist's satisfied face it seemed the picture had turned out as intended. Pinkie saw Kati looking at her and explained her drawing with gestures to match.

"I'm drawing my father and my brother, Pie. Hrmph! They like each other so much, they dumped me with Mama and ran away to live with Grandma and father's new girlfriend. Take this! And this! And this! Now I'm making them look really ugly and horrible. . . ."

Kati felt sorry for the white sheet of paper that was the recipient of Pinkie's anger. But then again, maybe it was good for Pinkie to be able to express her anger and not keep it pent up inside. But if Kati had those colored pencils in her hand, she doubted that her picture would have looked such a mess. Her own heart seemed to harbor no such anger.

On the way home Kati asked Aunt Da, "Did Mother hate Father?"

Aunt Da was startled. She bent down to look at Kati's face and answered, "Your mother never spoke of your father to me and I never asked, because I only knew your mother afterward. But I don't think your mother hated anyone. Especially anyone who helped her bring you into the world! Your mother loved you so, so much—she used to say all the time that you meant everything to her."

If she had some colored pencils, Kati would have drawn Mother in a beautiful pink gown with clear wings holding a wand like a fairy. Kati truly believed that by now Mother was happy in a new world, and that in the future they would meet again.

24

🪷

The Swing
*The happiness of those around
us is our happiness, too.*

The terrace garden on the ninth floor was truly
beautiful. When Kati stepped out of the lift with
Uncle Kunn, it was hard to believe that she was
high up in a skyscraper in a big city. A blue swimming pool appeared before them. Long deck-
chairs with white cushions were scattered round
the pool, and beach umbrellas with a blue-and-
white-striped pattern shaded various nooks and
corners. A path led toward an open wooden
pavilion, over which a *kanpai mahidol* vine had
grown, boasting blossoms of pink and white.

Kati had not yet made up her mind whether she should first explore the garden or jump into the pool to cool off when a glass door opened on her left, emitting a blast of cold air and a smell of lemon grass oil.

A woman in a white coat walked out and raised her hands together to greet Kunn in the Thai way. She smiled at Kati. Uncle Kunn bent down. "Touk knew Pat really well . . ." Touk finished the sentence for him. "I was Pat's masseuse. I gave her massages from before she was sick right until . . . until she moved to Hua Hin."

Touk's eyes grew moist. "Pat spoke of her little girl so often I felt I knew you. Be a good girl, won't you, dear—it would make your mom so happy not to have to worry about you. And if there's anything I can do for you, Kunn, just let me know. Pat was very helpful to me, and I will never forget her."

Afterward, Uncle Kunn told Kati that Touk's husband had been addicted to gambling. He gambled everything they had. Touk separated from him and had to bring up her son on her own. Kati's mother had helped out many times, especially with school fees. It seemed that Mother had done a great deal to make those around her happy. Kati felt proud to be her mother's daughter.

The little swing was half-hidden under a trellis overgrown with vines. Uncle Kunn had gone swimming in the pool. Kati walked all around and came to a stop in front of the swing. Swinging up in the air on top of that tall building had a curious effect, as though you were swinging up to touch the clouds. Kati let her feelings go with the breeze. The view of the capital city looked strange and new to her eyes. Her thoughts returned to the envelope that Uncle Dong had handed her that afternoon.

The envelope had been addressed in Mother's handwriting. The person to whom the letter was addressed was none other than Kati's father. Uncle Dong said that just by slipping this letter in a postbox, Kati would get to meet her father.

Kati missed her mother so much. Mother

had prepared everything for Kati but had been willing to leave the final decision for Kati to make for herself.

The swing flew higher and higher. Post the letter. Don't post the letter. Post the letter. Don't post the letter. Kati chanted to herself to the rhythm of the swing.

But she already knew what she wanted to do. It was how she was to do it that required some thought.

25

Postbox
All I ask is to be happy at heart.

A letter cannot be posted without a stamp. What Uncle Dong had said was wrong. If Kati wanted to send Mother's letter, she would need to go to the post office, which was not far from their apartment—five minutes' walk at the most.

Kati knew everyone was intently waiting for her decision, even though no one mentioned it or tried to hurry her in any way. They all appeared to be very nervous, but seemed to be doing their best not to pressure her.

When Kati was ready, she came out of her bedroom and told Aunt Da she wanted to go to the post office. Aunt Da, Uncle Kunn, and Uncle Dong all jumped to their feet, exactly like the time Tong sat down on the red ants' nest at the foot of the mango tree. In other circumstances Kati would have laughed, because all three grown-ups seemed at a complete loss as to what to do next. Finally, Uncle Dong cleared his throat and said that actually he had to go to the shops as well, so he would walk there with Kati. Uncle Kunn mumbled that perhaps he could go too to help carry the shopping, as it might be too much for Uncle Dong at his age. Any other time Uncle Dong would have raised the ceiling with rage, as no one was allowed to get away with pointed remarks about aging or senior citizens to Uncle Dong's face.

So it was that four figures followed one another into the lift in single file, spreading out four abreast when they reached the lane. Kati stood stock-still when she reached the post office and turned to face the others. She

said, "I'd like to go in by myself, please."
"Fine!" three voices answered in a chorus of
varying pitches.

Kati walked into the post office and joined
a queue before the counter. She gave the letter
to the clerk. After she had paid the money,
Kati received the stamps, which she pasted
onto the envelope. She posted the letter in the
postbox.

Now only the postbox knew her secret.
Kati looked at the slot through which you
posted the letters. She had the feeling it was
winking at her as if they had some under-
standing between them. Kati smiled and
walked out to join the little committee that
awaited her.

From that moment on, the life of the house
in the city was heavy with waiting. People started
when the phone rang and then argued over who
was going to pick it up. There were three or four
trips a day downstairs to check the mail. Kati
couldn't help laughing because, as the postal
clerk had told her, letters to the British Isles took
at least four days. Then again, who could say

how keen the recipient would be to reply? Most importantly, Mother had left instructions that if there was no reply within seven days, they were to return to the house on the water.

Kati didn't let the time pass only in waiting. She cajoled Uncle Kunn into taking her to the planetarium, to the science museum, and finally to an astronomy camp organized by the university science faculty.

What a shame that the city sky was so full of pollution that you couldn't see the constellations, but Kati was content to simply study the night sky. It made her feel good, and she promised herself that she would do it more often. The universe was so vast; what kind of power over it could puny little humans possibly have? Gazing into the sky made one feel humble. It made your proudest ambitions dissolve into the ether, leaving only a little heart beating in a breast that tried its best to protect itself and find happiness where it could, not craving the impossible, not wanting things beyond its reach.

Kati was too young to camp out overnight

in the tent with the university students, but Uncle Kunn allowed her to spend the best part of the night with the other stargazers, returning home close to dawn.

She fell asleep in the car and woke only when she was being carried up to bed. She pretended to be asleep and lay, not moving, on the bed while Aunt Da firmly tucked her in.

"Tomorrow time's up, right, Da? Will she be sad if there's no response?"

"She probably will, but what can we do about it?" Aunt Da stroked Kati's hair. Her voice trembled. Kati was about to open her eyes and confess the truth when she heard Uncle Dong's voice say, "Kati is Pat's daughter. She's not as fragile as we all think, you know. She is really doing very well. She certainly has all our love."

Uncle Dong had spoken words from Kati's heart. Kati turned over and went to sleep in an instant.

26

The Old Thai House
Leave the shadows of the past.

Kati's journey ended when the car stopped in front of the house on the water. This really was the end of her adventures in the big wide world, where she'd had to be a detective and unravel a mystery, just like in the books she'd read. Once Mother had said that we were all like characters in a story who encountered various challenges, which, once passed, conferred a new depth of emotional experience and made you a fuller person for having experienced them. You looked at the world differently from then on. Mother liked to use big words with Kati. They sounded good, even though they were sometimes hard to understand, but at this moment Kati felt that she really had grown up a lot more.

Grandma and Grandpa's embrace was as warm and safe as Kati had remembered. There could be no happier place than home, and the house on the water was truly Kati's home.

The house had a long history stretching back to Kati's great-grandfather. Grandpa had told her that once it was an old-fashioned Thai house, big, beautiful, and spacious, renowned throughout the village. It had been carefully built and crafted, complete with sleeping quarters, children's quarters, a lofty hall for receiving guests, a kitchen, and a long gallery in which to hang birdcages—all joined by an open veranda, shaded by big trees: mango, jackfruit, and chempaka.

With the passing of time, everything had deteriorated, until the old Thai house had become shabby and dilapidated. Grandpa had used his savings to renovate it extensively, sparing no cost and reducing it to a single house where it was possible to live comfortably. The handiwork of the modern builders was not as good as the builders of old, but they had persevered and retained as many of the original features as possible: the ample slanting eaves and carved windbreaks, the gable paneled in a traditional crisscross pattern.

Kati loved everything about this house. She was content with all she had here, and now there were no more lost or discarded pieces of her life to find.

She sat by the pier. In her heart she greeted the water, the trees, and the sunlight around her. Grandpa walked over to sit beside her and catch her once again in a tight hug as though he had not shown his love for her sufficiently with the last hug.

"At the temple they said the abbot will be back next week. I guess Tong will get back just in time for the new school term."

Kati counted the days in her heart. There were still a number of days before Tong and his uncle, the abbot, would start to travel home.

Tong had said he would be following his uncle on the itinerary arranged by their hosts. But he would end up at the temple on the hill where he had stayed when they first arrived, the temple whose address Tong had given Kati.

"Grandma wants to make a big merit offering at the local temple, but she wants to wait for the abbot to get back. That's good. Grandma needs something to look forward to right now. I hear she's going to cook up a storm, with her usual creative cooking. Creative—sure! Creating work for other people, don't you know?" Grandpa laughed at his own joke.

It was true. Kati saw a huge pile of coconuts under the house, and there were bananas drying on a big tray. A jar with pickled mangoes hid behind the water jar. Grandma had not been idle. Kati felt that the atmosphere at home was no longer completely grief-stricken, though in Grandma's and Grandpa's eyes she could see the shadow of that recent farewell.

But the pain and fear of that inevitable event, which they wished desperately to forestall, was gone.

What Grandpa said was true. Looking forward was the best thing to do.

Epilogue

Tomorrow was the first day of term for the new school year. Kati would be glad to see her friends again, but today she had something else to be happy about, because early in the morning Tong had rowed Uncle Abbot over to receive the alms offerings. As the bow of the boat appeared round a bend in the waterway, the sound of oars hitting water broke through the still mist, which was just beginning to evaporate after the departing night's dew. Tong's smile evoked answering smiles in all who saw him, just as it always had.

Grandpa laughed and called out his greeting: "Hey, so how's the American boy—how'd you like your taste of life abroad, hey?"

Tong raised his hands in his usual deep *wai* greeting, but only smiled in response. Grandpa turned to Uncle Abbot, and Kati heard them fixing the date for the merit offering. Grandma had instructed Grandpa not to forget to ask what day suited the abbot. If Grandpa had failed to do so, both he and Kati would have ended up with serious indigestion, as Grandma would most certainly have complained all through breakfast.

Tong said he had something for Kati. It was a book on stargazing, a big hardcover with beautiful colored pictures. As if he knew what she was thinking, Tong reassured Kati that it wasn't too expensive. He had wanted to bring back all the beautiful books he saw overseas, but he didn't have enough room in his luggage. Kati thanked Tong and watched him as he rowed the boat away.

Kati had to wait all day for a chance to look at the astronomy book, and by the time she opened the book, it was dark. She wanted to know if the sky she could see from here was the same as the one shown in the book, but she hadn't even started spelling out the English words when she found a sheet of paper between the first pages of the book. Actually, it wasn't paper; it was a post-card of the night sky somewhere. Kati's name and address was written clearly on the back in Tong's handwriting. There was even a stamp on it.

Hi, Kati,
I meant to send this in the mail, but then I thought it'd be more fun to copy someone else I know and not post it. Thanks for the letter, and thanks for giving me a part to play in your story. Whatever your decision, you've done the right thing. I'm sure of that. I have heaps to tell you. But that'll have to wait till I see you again, okay?
Tong (Suwan)

Tong's handwriting was of the kind that Thai people say is as large and round as cook-ing pots. It was a wonder he had managed to squeeze in so many sentences in that tiny space. Kati was glad Tong had understood her and not been cross at what she'd done.

That night Kati opened the old biscuit tin where she kept special things and put Tong's card in with Mother's letter: the letter Mother had written to Father, the letter that Kati had decided not to post. That day Kati had sent a letter overseas, but it had been the letter to Tong. This had saved Kati from having to explain to Uncle Dong and Uncle Kunn and Aunt Da what she had decided and why.

Sometimes life did not lend itself to explanations. Hadn't Mother said that? As for Kati and Mother, Kati knew her mother understood, and there was no need for explanations.

Kati bowed to the Buddha before she went to bed. Tomorrow morning she would have to wake early for school. Everything was the way it always had been. Nothing had changed. And tomorrow the clatter of Grandma's spatula would wake Kati from her slumber to greet the world again.